Tim Minchin's
i Grow UP

Illustrated by Steve Antony

SCHOLASTIC

When I grow up, I will be **tall** enough to reach the branches that I have to reach to climb the trees you get to climb

when you're grown-up.

And when I grow up, I will be **smart** enough to answer all the questions

that you need to know the answers to before you're grown-up.

And when I grow up, I will

eat sweets every day on the way to work, and I...

...will go to bed late every night.

And I will wake up when the sun comes up and I...

...will watch cartoons

until my eyes go

square, and I won't **care,** 'cause I'll be all grown up when I grow up.

When
I
grow
up...

grow up...

When I grow up...

I will be **strong** enough
to carry all the heavy things
you have to haul around with you
when you're a grown-up.

And when I grow up, I will be **brave** enough to fight the creatures

that you have to **fight**

beneath your bed each night

to be a grown-up.

And when I grow up, I will have treats **every day...**

...and I'll **play** with **things**

that mums pretend that mums
don't think are fun.

And I will **wake up** when the sun comes up
and I will spend all day just
lying in the sun

and I won't burn 'cause I'll be all grown up
when I grow up.

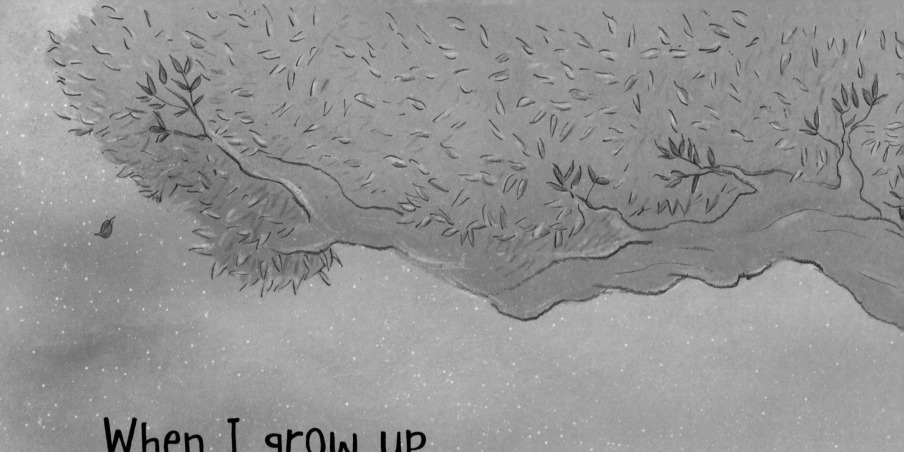

When I grow up.

When I grow up.

When I grow up.